HONEY

ISHA MELLOR

HONEY

ILLUSTRATED BY
RODNEY SHACKELL

Congdon & Lattès
New York
1981

Copyright © 1980 by Isha Mellor
Illustrations copyright © 1980 by W.H. Allen & Co. Ltd.

Published by Congdon & Lattès, Inc.
Distributed by St. Martin's Press

First published in England by W. H. Allen & Co. Ltd., 1980

Library of Congress Cataloging in Publication Data

Mellor, Isha.
Honey.

Reprint of the ed. published by W.H. Allen, London.
1. Honey.   2. Honey (in religion, folklore, etc.)
3. Cookery (Honey)   I. Title.
SF539.M38   1981   641.3'8   80-28499
Publisher's ISBN 0-86553-018-1
Distributor's ISBN 0-312-92306-6

Acknowledgements

Michael Yeats for the lines from "The Lake Isle of Innisfree" in *Collected Poems*.

David Higham Associates Limited for the lines from *Under Milk Wood*, published by J. M. Dent.

E.P. Dutton & Co., Inc. for the lines from *Winnie-the-Pooh*. Copyright © 1926 by E.P. Dutton & Co., Inc. Copyright Renewal © 1954 by A.A. Milne.

St. George Book Service, Spring Valley, New York, for quotation from *Nine Lectures on Bees* by Rudolf Steiner, published by St. George Publications, 1975.

Allen (George) & Unwin Limited for extract from *The Life of the Bee* by Maurice Maeterlinck.

Donald Marston, Chairman of the Inner London Beekeepers Association, who kindly checked the facts contained in the manuscript.

Contents

Introduction 8

Ancient Britain 11

Antiquity 12

Art 14

Beauty 15

Beekeepers 18

Beeswax 21

The Bible 23

Bumble Bees 24

Cancer 25

Constituents 27

Countries of origin 28

Diets 31

Dreams 33

Endearments 34

Exhibition 35

Flowers 38

Habit 40

Hierarchy 41

Honey bear 43

Honey guide 44

Honey-mouthed 44

Honey stone 45

Honeydew 45

Honeymoon 46

Honeypot 46

Lore 47

Maeterlinck 50

Mead 51

Nectar 53

Bee orchid 54

Plant cures 55

Pollen & hayfever 57

Propolis 58

Purity 60

"The Queen Bee" (Grimm) 61

Recipes 64

Royal jelly 70

Shakespeare's hive 71

Shopping for honey 73

Singing hinny 73

Smoking 74

Statistics 74

Rudolph Steiner 75

Stings 77

Storage 77

Survival 78

Sweet tooth 79

Introduction

Honey—a lovely word, a cozy word. It conjures up images of quality, of caring. We remember kind aunts spreading it for us on good brown bread and butter, and how the teeth crunched slightly as we bit into it, or what fun it was to let the runny kind swoop from one side of the slice to the other. Even as adults we may have a caring person at hand to bring us a glass of hot water with honey and lemon or whisky, to calm a sore throat and guarantee a quiet night. We remember Pooh as a top furry favorite, humming his hums and gourmandizing over honey.

Honey was almost the only source of sweetening in ancient, and not so ancient times, if one considers that it is only in the last 200 years that refined sugar became cheap enough for general use. There are records of the harvesting and use of honey all over the world. These appear in the form of legends, cave paintings, literature, and technical and philosophical studies of the present day. Honey is generally the first image that springs to mind when we need an example of sweetness or a term of endearment.

Obviously, one cannot consider honey on its own. The bees who produce it so miraculously must come into the picture, particularly when one is told that if every bee in the world were to be wiped out, life as we know it would screech to a halt within six years. The reason for such a catastrophe would presumably be the withdrawal of the pollination service provided by bees, and the consequent failure of plant life for feeding purposes. A terrible prospect.

Many will declare that one lifetime is not sufficient for the study of these creatures who inhabit a microcosm run with superlative efficiency and devotion—the hive. Man may learn many lessons from bees, and while his curiosity about them continues, there is hope for world sanity.

The many instances in which bees are considered to be holy, highlight the respect that man has always had for honey, that food ready for the taking. It is, with milk, one of the two natural products that exist purely as food, with no further preparation necessary. However honey is analyzed, there remains a part of it that is a mystery, and it is this mystery that we instinctively experience when we eat the merest spoonful.

The following pages attempt to bring together various aspects of honey: its contribution to nutrition, healing, science, literature, art, and the many myths and customs surrounding it. But when one starts to consider honey, there is no doubt that one is going to be as busy as any busy bee!

Ancient Britain

Ancient Britain was always being invaded or visited, for one reason or another. When the Phoenicians came to trade for lead and tin, they observed how prominently honey featured in the diet of the inhabitants, and they called the land the Isle of Honey.

Druid bards called it the Honey Isle of Beli. Beli was the British name for Bile, the hero of Celtic culture.

By the time the Romans landed, every village kept bees in hives, mostly woven from osier, and bee-keeping was quite an industry. Plutarch wrote about

the amazing longevity of the natives who seemed to show signs of age only at 120. Pliny the Elder commented on the amount of honey brew that was drunk.

Antiquity

They told her how, upon St Agnes' Eve,
Young virgins might have visions of delight,
And soft adorings from their loves receive
Upon the honey'd middle of the night,
If ceremonies due they did aright.

The Eve of St Agnes,
John Keats

Ancient Egyptians used honey as an embalming material, and Democritus and Alexander the Great are two well-known characters who were buried in coatings of honey. In Burma all bodies were steeped in honey to preserve them until money for the prolonged funeral rites could be found. In the interests of economy, this honey was scraped off afterwards and sold in the markets. Honey was incorruptible, so where was the harm?

Hippocrates, the father of medicine, had a recipe for an aphrodisiac made with ass's meat, milk, and honey, and nearer our time honey was fed to the inmates of the harems of Istanbul for the furthering of their prime activity. Brides and bridegrooms in the

Balkans used to have their faces smeared with honey, and Magyars are said to have gone so far as to spread it on the sexual organs of girls and boys to ensure their popularity with the opposite sex.

Homer mentions a pottage of barley-meal, honey, wine, and grated goats' milk cheese, that must have had an interesting taste. Apicius, the Roman cookery expert, recorded that turnips were a cheap form of food for country folk and could be preserved with myrtle berries in vinegar and honey.

A near disastrous effect of honey was related by Xenophon when a 10,000-strong Greek army was retreating from Persia. They consumed honey from hives near an abundance of *Rhododendron ponticum*, and were beset by such terrible vomiting and flux that they were unable to stand. Fortunately, they recovered after three days.

Roman soldiers carried honey in their packs for use in treating their wounds.

Art

Early cave paintings are to be found that depict beekeepers at work, and one of these can be clearly seen near Bicorp in Spain. They appear in Africa, and on the east colonnade of the tomb of Pa-bu-sa at Thebes. The British Museum has a Greek vase dating from about 540 BC that is decorated with a scene of intruders in a Cretan cave being attacked by bees.

Strangely, bees do not feature very much in later art. The London National Gallery contains only one notable example, and even here the bees are kept to the bottom left-hand corner of the work. It is the enchanting picture by Lucas Cranach the Elder—who lived from 1472 to 1553—entitled *Cupid Complaining to Venus*. It depicts Venus, naked but for a plaited necklace and a splendid Ascot hat of ostrich feathers, standing under a fruiting apple tree. A chubby, winged Cupid looks up at her, more worried and appealing than complaining, holding a honeycomb that he has obviously plucked from a slit in the tree trunk. All about him angry bees are swarming, and his only hope from a nasty lot of stings lies in intervention by the Goddess.

A late 15th century painter, Piero di Cosimo, created a picture with the title *The Discovery of Honey*. It is a scene of tremendous rioting and drunken joy among humans and satyrs. Presumably they lost no time in finding out how to make mead!

In 1968 Michael Ayrton, the writer and artist, made a golden sculpture that he copied from the original by Daedalus, the legendary craftsman for the Temple of Aphrodite. He gave it the simple name *The Golden Honeycomb*.

Beauty

Honey spot is the name for a mole on the skin.

In the past, most beauty preparations were concocted at home from various beneficial ingredients to be found in the house and garden. Preservation was always a problem, so fresh batches would be made frequently for safety reasons. Nowadays, the public has no way of knowing how long a cream or lotion has been in the shop, the contents deteriorating and becoming harmful.

One of the chief ingredients, with wax, of homemade beauty aids was, and still is, honey. The darker the honey the better its mineral content, the property that rejuvenates exhausted tissues. Because honey is able to hold moisture it is very good for dry skin, and it can also draw out dirt from the pores. The valuable vitamins it contains play an important part in maintaining skin health, both when applied externally and when eaten as part of a regular diet.

Applying honey direct to the skin, while being

really beneficial, can be a daunting job. However, it is well worth persevering, and if the fingers are first dipped in warm water it becomes much easier to pat the honey onto face and neck.

If one takes a calculating look at the glossily advertised and over-packaged commercial beauty products, it does seem an extravagance to buy these tinted and perfumed aids. One has also to confront those lacquered damsels behind the counters, who appear to be above the sordid procedure of selling but who, once started, will charm every penny out of one's purse. No wonder many women stick to the old soap and water treatment! For them, natural creams and lotions are the answer, and there is now no need to mess about making them at home unless you wish. There are entirely reliable firms which do the job for you. One such is Hylda Conway, who manufactures Honeydew Cosmetics.

For those who find satisfaction in do-it-yourself activities, here are some recipes for honey beauty treatments:

Face packs 1 teaspoon honey
     1 teaspoon glycerine
     1 raw egg yolk

     1 teaspoon honey
     1 teaspoon sour cream
     1 raw egg yolk

     1 teaspoon honey
     1 teaspoon lemon juice or
      apple cider vinegar
     Good for oily skin

     1 teaspoon honey
     Beaten egg white
     Apply to loose skin around eyes, but for no more than twenty minutes

Hand lotion 1 dessertspoon honey
     1 dessertspoon glycerine
     2 tablespoons witch hazel
     2 tablespoons vegetable oil
     Dissolve in a little warm water
     Add 1 dessertspoon fine oatmeal

It is quite often related by the mother of a teenage child how, in desperation, she tried the honey cure on acne—that distressing skin condition. At least it could do no harm, she thought. But cure it did, as if by magic. Perhaps magic is the word for honey's ability to draw out moisture, kill bacteria, and remain self-sterile. Magic or science, it works.

Beekeepers

I will arise and go now, and go to Innisfree,
And a small cabin build there, of clay and
*   wattles made:*
Nine bean-rows will I have there, a hive for the
*   honey-bee,*
And live alone in the bee-loud glade.

> The Lake Isle of Innisfree,
> *William Butler Yeats*

No one should take up beekeeping without first getting advice from experts. This can best be obtained from a beekeeping association or club, and it will be a matter of surprise to discover how many of these exist both in country areas and in towns.

Those about to retire will be well advised to consider beekeeping as an occupation during the years that are so often spent in an armchair, knowing that one ought to be elsewhere doing something useful.

But it should be taken up early in retirement, since it becomes so very absorbing. It needs little space, and a minimum of equipment costing in the region of $75.00. Membership in an association will qualify one for discounts in the price of such equipment, in addition to free advice and stocks of bees.

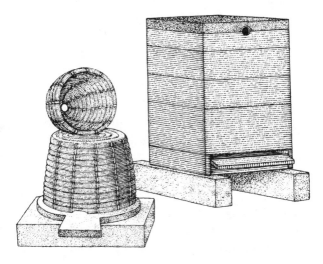

It is not necessary for a beekeeper to live in the country or even to have a garden, for in towns as large and heavily polluted as London there are gardens, parks, and tree-lined streets to provide the essential nectar for foraging bees. Rooftops and balconies can become ideal sites for hives, and it is interesting to learn that London beekeepers often carry off top awards in honey shows and contests.

Beehives kept in a private garden will not cause neighbor trouble if they are properly looked after by their keeper so that the bees do not develop delinquent and aggressive habits!

An ideal position for a hive is in an orchard in bloom, and most orchard owners will be happy to act as landlords to a bee colony in return for the wonderful pollination service the fruit trees will receive. Growers of Cox's Orange Pippins are foremost in actually paying for hives to be placed on their land.

Women generally make ideal beekeepers. They have the right touch, steady and gentle. It is essential to have no fear, and to exercise a tactful caution when handling bees. A reassuring tone of voice is also a help.

Beeswax

Wax is produced from special glands under a bee's body, and from it are made the honeycombs to contain the three kinds of eggs and the honey. The cells are such miracles of accuracy that it has often been suggested that the hexagons should be used as official measures. The honey cells are cleverly tilted slightly backwards so that the honey does not ever run out with the force of gravity. Beeswax will not melt at any temperature under 140 F, so is safe from any earthly weather temperatures.

In the past it was considered to be more important than honey itself, and today it commands a higher price than this wonderful food. It is easy to understand what an impact was made by the introduction of beeswax for candle making, so much sweeter and cleaner than tallow and the primitive rush lights. The

Roman Catholic Church has always used beeswax for its candles. Old religious laws insisted that they had to be 100% pure, but economy has relaxed this strict rule, so that 25% is now the required proportion.

Candles were made by the dipping method or by pouring melted wax over and over a wick. The Worshipful Company of Wax Chandlers is still an important guild, and has undertaken to supply candles in perpetuity for the new high altar of St. Paul's Cathedral after bombing damage in 1940.

The faces and hands of Madame Tussaud's models are formed from 75% beeswax because it gives the right translucent quality of skin. The original Madame was the niece of a Swiss doctor who owned a display of waxen figures. She took up the craft and later had the task of making death masks of guillotine victims during the French Revolution, her most famous ones being Marie Antoinette and Louis XVI.

The uses of beeswax are legion. It is used by dentists for making impressions, and in clinics for hot wax applications to arthritic hands and feet. It forms the base of zinc and castor oil ointment—used on babies' nether regions. Tough stitching that has to last is made of waxed thread, so it is used by sailmakers, cobblers, and tailors. Ropes are dressed with it, and machinery that is exposed to sea water. It forms the base of most lipsticks and many other cosmetics. With turpentine it has always been the best furniture polish, and even in this age of aerosols it is still of use because of its great solubility.

So once again, it can be seen that man has cause to be grateful to bees that work so hard to produce both honey and wax. To give 1 lb. of wax a bee has to consume 5 to 10 lbs. of honey.

The Bible

And I am come down to deliver them out of the hand of the Egyptians, and to bring them up out of that land unto a good land flowing with milk and honey.

Exodus, iii. 8.

And he said unto them, Out of the eater came forth meat, and out of the strong came forth sweetness. And they could not in three days expound the riddle . . . And the men of the city said unto him on the seventh day before the sun went down, What is sweeter than honey? and what is stronger than a lion?

Judges, xv. 14 & 18.

Behold, a virgin shall conceive, and bear a son, and shall call his name Immanuel.
Butter and honey shall he eat, that he may know to refuse the evil, and choose the good.

Isaiah, vii. 14.

The judgments of the Lord are true and righteous altogether. More to be desired are they than gold, yea, than much fine gold: sweeter also than honey, and the honeycomb. *Psalms*, xix. 10.

And the same John had his raiment of camel's hair, and a leathern girdle about his loins; and his meat was locusts and wild honey. *Matthew*, iii. 4.

And when he had thus spoken, he shewed them His hand and His feet.

And while they yet believed not for joy, and wondered, He said unto them, Have ye here any meat? And they gave Him a piece of a broiled fish, and of an honeycomb. *Luke*, xxiv. 41.

Bumble bees

Bumble bees attract from us a kind of loving curiosity. We seem to have no fear of them because they make a lovely sound, have generously furry bodies, and, we believe, no stings. Actually, some of them do have stings and are known to use them on us, though infrequently.

They produce only enough honey for their own consumption and to store for seeing them through a few days of bad weather. They do not give the human race any benefits of their foraging industry. The whole colony, except the young queen, dies every autumn.

They have extra long tongues which are able to reach the nectar in certain flowers, such as red clover, which lies out of reach of the ordinary honey bee; and with their superior strength can enter the tight-lipped snapdragon flower, making it easier for the smaller creature to get inside later on.

Cancer

Innumerable books are written on the advantages of using honey both internally and externally for reasons of health. A look at the index of any of these books will show that there is scarcely a disease or malfunction that cannot benefit from treatment with honey: arthritis, bronchitis, cancer, diabetes, goiter, insomnia, neuritis, enlargement of the prostate— right down to wounds. And if there is an illness beginning with Z, then it will surely figure in such an index!

Naturally, one turns to the pages dealing with the particular disorder that may bother one, but the disease most widely feared, and for which fresh treatment is constantly sought, is cancer. Medical authorities generally lay stress on prevention that can be effected by eating natural foods. Processed and preserved food should be avoided whenever possible. Honey rates as one of the topmost examples on the list of natural foods, and it is interesting to speculate on the fact that, particularly in heather honey, radium is present.

This fact was first discovered in 1908 by a French chemist called Alin Caillas. When he filled glass tubes with honey and placed them on photographic plates he found, after a month, that there were impressions made by radiation. This was surely an important discovery, but it seems that there has been no follow-up to it since that day, apart from the discovery that acid soils, on which heather freely grows, retain radium. Heather honey is thixotropic (a jelly that liquifies when stirred, like non-drip paints), and is in this respect different from all other honeys —a fact that adds further to the mystery of honey.

There is a belief that no beekeeper ever suffers from cancer, and there is speculation that this idea should be added to the fact that in any scientific analysis of honey there remains a 3% area that defies classification. This might make for an illuminating line of research.

In 1955 an eminent British surgeon gave an account of his treatment of an ulcerating area of skin surrounding a radical excision of a breast carcinoma. There was a deep cavity, and into this he packed granulated honey every day, covering it with dry gauze. The result was a speedy cleansing and healing. Honey is non-irritant, non-toxic, self-sterile, bactericidal, nutritive, cheap, easily obtained, easily applied, and effective, according to this enterprising man. What more could one want?

Constituents

The *Encyclopedia Britannica* gives a straightforward explanation of what honey is: "A sweet, viscous liquid food, dark golden in colour, produced in honey sacs of various bees from the nectar of flowers . . . The nectar is ripened into honey by inversion of the major portion of its sucrose sugar into the sugars levulose (fructose) and dextrose (glucose) and by the removal of excess moisture."

But scientists want to go further, and they have analyzed honey to break it down into its constituents and calculate the proportions. But always there is something that eludes them. Here is a list of the known content of honey: water, levulose, dextrose, sucrose, dextrin, higher sugars, nitrogen, proteins, wax, plant acids, salts, residues (resins, gums, pollen, etc.), vitamins.

But the real secret of the recipe remains with the bees. After all, chemists have synthesized all the substances they have discovered in honey, yet the result is *not* honey. What is it that the bees put in? Where lies the magic of honey?

Countries of origin

Bees were the emblem of the Bonapartes in France

From olden times, Hymettus honey has been noted for its flavor, derived from the nectar of the wild thyme growing on the slopes of this mount lying to the east of Athens. The same plant flourishing near Mount Hybla in Sicily produced a honey frequently mentioned by poets.

In America the only indigenous honey bee is the stingless variety (*Meliponinae*) that was domesticated to a certain extent by the Maya in sub-tropical regions. Productive beekeeping started with bees carried there by European colonists in their ships during the 17th century.

It is interesting to note that the State of Utah is today known as The Beehive State. When the Mormons first went there they brought with them the deseret or honey bee, and wanted to name their state Deseret when incorporated into the Union. Their seal consists of a beehive surrounded by flowers and above that, the word INDUSTRY.

It is difficult to believe that honey bees are not indigenous to Australia or New Zealand, both so well known for their honey. Black bees from Europe are thought to have arrived in Australia on the convict ship *Isabella* in 1822. Missionaries are credited with having taken bees from Australia to New Zealand in 1839. Later, in 1862, Italian bees were exported to Australia from Exeter in England on a voyage that took seventy-nine days.

In a way, the importation of honey bees to these countries was an advantage, because the beekeepers then had at their disposal a great deal of advanced technical knowledge, and they were not prejudiced by ancient methods and rituals that tended to hold back sensible production in many other countries of the world.

Today it is fair to say that there is hardly a country that does not produce honey for its own consumption. Where this is not sufficient, it is possible to import it from nations with very large outputs, such as North America, USSR, China, South and Central America, and Europe—all with over 100,000 tons a year.

Consumers have become connoisseurs, demanding and buying the honey they fancy from high-class grocers and specialty shops. Others look for price bargains as well as quality. Thus we are able to buy jars bearing labels from numerous countries, such as Mexico, Jamaica, Argentina, Canada, Greece, Spain, Poland, Hungary, Australia, New Zealand, to name but a few. A honey addict will generally pay a good price for the product of his choice, and bear it home with joy at having the best food in the world.

Diets

We are all free to choose the diet that appeals to us when we wish to shed excess weight or prevent fat from adding itself to our already adequate amount of flesh. It is impossible to convince anyone devoted to a low calorie diet that the low carbohydrate one is better, or vice versa; but whatever one's preference, it is wise to maintain a proper balance and not to carry any slimming diet to the point of starvation. Even a day or two of strict denial soon loses its effect when one reverts to normal eating.

The hardest deprivation is that of sweet foods, with the resultant lack of energy. This is where honey can play an important role. It is quickly absorbed into the bloodstream because it has been pre-digested by the bees. It has the added advantage of maintaining the level of energy and not setting up a continued longing for more sugar.

For those who count their calories, it should be known that 1 lb. of honey will provide 1,290 calories, or the equivalent of 6 pints of milk, 30 eggs, or 12 lbs. of apples. It is hard to imagine that anyone would wish to consume a whole pound of honey; it is best taken in small daily quantities, as one would a condiment, thus maintaining a sensible sugar level. A calorie-conscious dieter can work out, as any other dieter, the role that honey can play in daily consumption.

Followers of the low carbohydrate diet will know that a tablespoon of honey clocks up seventeen grams of carbohydrate. A tablespoon is really quite a large portion, enough to cover amply two slices of wholewheat bread (twenty-two grams). Of course, it has to be calculated whether those twenty-two grams are permitted! But in a total daily allowance of sixty, it should not be difficult to fit in a pleasant dose of sweetness.

There is a very nice fruit slimming diet that may be carried out for two days only. It consists of the juice of two oranges and one lemon put into a large tumbler. To this is added a large teaspoon of liquid honey and a thinly sliced medium banana. After stirring, not beating, it is slowly eaten with a spoon. It takes a long time to finish, but this is one of the reasons for its satisfying effect. The same concoction, with no other food or drink, is taken three times a day. Results will be noted in the region of the waist and diaphragm, which is very good news.

Dreams

Hide me from day's garish eye,
While the bee, with honied thigh,
That at her flowery work doth sing,
And the waters murmuring,
With such consort as they keep,
Entice the dewy-feather'd sleep.

Il Pensoroso,
John Milton

A dream of honey is a sign of suddenly being able to overcome a problem. It also predicts domestic and social sweetness.

In India it is an unhappy augury to experience a dream about honey.

If one dreams of a beehive, this foretells prosperity and freedom from worry. But if the hive is upset or the bees are let out, then there will be trouble of one's own making.

Even if bees sting one in a dream, they are still lucky signs. However, if they are dead it is a signal to beware of putting too much trust in friends.

If the bees are heard to buzz, good news is in the offing.

When a king dreams of breaking and eating from a honeycomb, it means that his people will bring him happiness and wealth.

Endearments

Honey people is a friendly name given to bees

We accept that Americans are the prime users of honey as a term of endearment. Honeychild, honey-lamb, honeybunch, honeypie are just a few instances. More often the plain word honey is used.

There is a story of the American couple staying in one of the identical rooms of a huge modern hotel. One evening the husband went out for a walk, leaving the room key with his wife. On his return he simply could not recall the number of their room. He went gently knocking on various doors, calling, "Honey! Are you there, Honey?" One angry response he received was, "What the hell do you want? This is a bathroom, not a beehive." Enough to turn him right off using the endearment ever again!

A much earlier user of the name was Chaucer—some say the earliest recorded use. In *The Miller's Tale* he wrote how Absolon "this joly lovere" got himself ready to serenade his Alisoun, even having "kembd his heer," spoke beneath her window and gently asked, "What do ye, hony-comb, sweete Alisoun, My faire bryd, my sweete cynamome?"

In Shakespeare's *Henry V* the Hostess says to Pistol, "Prithee, honey-sweet husband, let me bring thee to Staines."

Honey is often used as a name in Ireland, and in Scotland and Northumbria as Hinny or Hinnie.

Exhibition

To visit a honey show or exhibition is to spend a truly golden hour. Glistening jars stand on long tables covered with white cloths. The honey in them is both clear and granulated, the colors ranging from pale cream to almost black. One thinks of the words gold, bronze, amber, yellow, toffee, caramel, sunshine—each applicable to this host of glowing containers. The stickiness is overlooked, well battened beneath the immaculate screw tops, behind the walls of glass.

The exhibitors construct pyramids and tower blocks of pots with labels bearing their names, and the region and blossom that have produced the honey.

Then small square wooden frames enclosing honeycombs stand stacked on end, so one may marvel at how such delicate structures can hold the honey so securely under the thin wafer-like cappings. Here is natural honey, the best that can be eaten. Some jars of liquid honey contain jagged slabs of honeycomb, offering a choice to the consumer.

All told, a layman finds it impossible to imagine how the judges will arrive at their award-giving decisions.

Such a show also has on display various by-products of the hive. There are bottles of alcoholic mead, metheglin, and melomel, also cakes of pure beeswax turned out of their molds and looking like blancmanges. Beeswax candles of all sizes, carved and plain, stand tall or lie like toy soldiers in rows.

A sweet-smelling area displays different cakes, breads, and elaborate sweetmeats, all containing honey, making it very difficult not to stretch out a hand to snatch a sampling.

There are sure to be stalls of beauty preparations made with a base of honey, and others with medicaments containing bee products such as pollen, wax, or propolis (Nature's antibiotic). There seems to be no ailment that cannot be treated by kind permission of the bees.

Elsewhere, the equipment and protective clothing for beekeepers can be inspected. Shelves of books are on sale, giving information on every aspect of bee-keeping and honey production.

And if one stops to ask a question of any exhibitor or committee member hovering like gigantic bees around the stacks of honey jars, the reply will be given with a smile that has a source of sweetness. One leaves the place feeling grateful to the nation's beekeepers, and determined to lead a more healthy life by remembering, for a start, to eat more honey.

Flowers

The moan of doves in immemorial elms,
And murmuring of innumerable bees.

The Princess,
Alfred Lord Tennyson

There is an English saying: "Where there is the best honey there is also the best wool." Naturally, where there is no ploughing of the land there will be flowers for the bees, and the pasture for sheep.

The bee does not know the part it plays in fertilization as it unknowingly carries surplus pollen on its body from flower to flower. Ever practical, Nature sees to it that sources of nectar in flowers are clearly signalled by colorful markings on petals. This is to be noted, for instance, in the yellow guidelines on dark pansies or the yellow eye of forget-me-nots. Bees are red color-blind, so tend to visit blue flowers most readily and eagerly.

The different flowers in which bees forage of course determine the appearance and flavor of the resulting honey. In the main, it comes from the vast amount of tree blossom, and then the wide mixture of flowers. When a particular flower is abundantly in season its flavor and scent will be almost exclusive. The prolific white clover results in a pale and subtly flavored honey. The West Indian product collected from tobacco growing regions will have an aroma of fresh tobacco in addition to a full and rich flavor. Early fruit blossom such as apple, pear, and hawthorn provide a delicious taste, likewise the later bramble. Lime honey is another favorite, but it can be spoiled in appearance by the inclusion of dark honeydew.

Heather honey is dark and strong, with that obtained from ling being a jelly that smells faintly of horses. Herbs that are in themselves of health value and have flowers attractive to bees, as the famous wild thyme of Greece, will always provide a honey for discerning consumers.

Common wild flowers, when allowed to flourish, are generally well foraged by bees, the favorites being speedwell, borage, mallow, mignonette, vipers bugloss, dandelion, convolvulus, figwort, sainfoin, and many more. Vegetables, when gone to flower, are also much favored.

In the garden, single flowers are the valuable ones, and those such as lavender, Michaelmas daisy, and dahlias provide sources of nectar at the low time of summer when many other flowers have spent themselves.

Another surprisingly useful flower is the rose-bay willow herb that grew on bomb sites and was nick-

named fireweed, and it still proves to be of prime importance for the busy London bees.

It has been thought that flowering plants growing abundantly and constantly in other countries should be transplanted to lands less florally rich, in order to establish greater sources of nectar for the honey industry. Unfortunately, this is not a successful undertaking, the reason being that bees are so closely connected with the flora of their own country that they have to work too hard to adapt themselves to processing foreign nectar. This has to do with the tongue lengths of various species of bee, and also the varying degrees of temperature at which nectar is produced in certain flowers.

Habit

Stands the Church clock at ten to three?
And is there honey still for tea?

The Old Vicarage, Grantchester,
Rupert Brooke

A hive moved even a few feet away from its original position will flummox its bees. They will circle the original place over and over again until they actually drop dead from exhaustion.

Hierarchy

All Nature seems at work. Slugs leave their lair—
The bees are stirring—birds are on the wing—
And Winter, slumbering in the open air,
Wears on his smiling face a dream of Spring!
And I, the while, the sole unbusy thing,
Nor honey make, nor pair, nor build, nor sing.

Work Without Hope,
Samuel Taylor Coleridge

Queen: She is the mother, laying up to 3,000 eggs a day during the height of summer. 1,500 eggs is the average amount. She will be spared all other chores, fed and groomed by her attendants. Although such a prolific matron, she has no interest in the rearing of her brood. She is an egg machine. Her diet of royal jelly was responsible for her growth into a queen, otherwise she would have developed into a worker.

She can have a lifespan of up to five years, but more commonly two.

A few of her eggs will be sealed in specially large cells so that they can grow into virgin queens, one of which will take her place. At about the time of the capping of these large cells the old queen will prepare to swarm out of the hive to start up a new colony. The first virgin queen to emerge will seek out and fight her sisters to the death. Between five and ten days later she will leave the hive to mate with drones on the nuptial flight, and after that return to start the egg production process all over again.

Drone: This is a male bee, born to lead an indolent life, also waited upon by the workers, until it flies out to meet and mate with a queen, quite often from another colony. Copulation means death for him, for his genitalia are torn out by the act and remain in the body of the queen. Surviving drones who do not succeed in mating return to the hive to fly out again another day. But at the end of the season, with winter approaching, these drones find a hostile reception waiting for them. They are no longer fed and are

42

even prevented from entering, so they die of starvation and exposure to cold night air.

Worker: Not surprisingly, this is a female. Her hard-working life lasts about six weeks, during which time she builds the combs from wax produced by her special glands, processes the honey after having collected nectar and pollen from flowers, regulates the temperature of the hive by vigorous wing fanning, and in the early part of her life acts as a house bee whose duties are to feed and groom the queen and clean the premises. Hers is a lifetime of service and devotion.

Honey bear

Isn't it funny
How a bear likes honey?
Buzz! Buzz! Buzz!
I wonder why he does?

Winnie-the-Pooh,
A.A. Milne

The honey bear of India wears a fur coat so thick that the stings of bees cannot penetrate it.

Honey guide

The black-throated honey guide (*Indicatoridae*) of the woodpecker family is an African bird that leads a cunningly organized life. It becomes very excited, emitting a *churr-churr* call when it sees honey-loving creatures such as man or the honey badger. Then it will fly ahead encouragingly and lead them to a bee's nest that it has previously discovered. Standing by until the predators have taken away the honey, the wily bird will say thank you and dart in to gobble the remaining wax upon which it simply dotes. Ornithologists, of course, do not credit it with such deliberate behavior.

The bird will respond to the smell of a burning candle, and it is recorded by a 16th century Portuguese missionary in Africa that his church candles often provided a meal for local honey guides.

Honey-mouthed

To be honey-mouthed is to be sweet or soft in speech, even to the point of insincerity. Shakespeare uses the term in *The Winter's Tale* when Paulina undertakes to tell the king that the queen has been early delivered of a daughter:

He must be told on't, and he shall: the office
Becomes a woman best. I'll take 't upon me.
If I prove honey-mouth'd, let my tongue blister.

Ogma, the Celtic god of literature, was also called
Cermait, which meant "the honey-mouthed."

Honey stone

Honey stone is the name given to melanite, which
when broken up and steeped in water will sweeten it.

Honeydew

"More flies are caught with honey than with vinegar,"
say the wise Dutch and also the French.

Anyone unfortunate enough to park a car under a
lime tree in summertime will not do so again. It will
be covered with a nasty stickiness. This is honeydew, and it is the result of the digestive process of
aphids that have been gorging themselves on the sap
of the leaves. Some people believe that honeydew is
actually produced by the leaves and that it then
attracts the aphids, but this is not so.

In Germany, a high-priced pine honey is made
from the honeydew that collects on those trees; but
the honeydew from limes will find its way into most
hives, and it has the effect of darkening the honey.

45

Honeymoon

Ancient Teutons extended their wedding festivities by carousing on honey wines such as mead, metheglin, or hydromel for thirty days. Poor Attila the Hun rather overdid this kind of celebration after his own marriage, and died.

This custom produced the name honeymoon for the holiday period enjoyed by newlyweds. This holiday could of course be shorter, and a 19th century wedding report stated: "The happy couple left town . . . to pass the honeyweek, for they had not time to make a moon of it."

Some claim that the term honeymoon began as a reference to the changing moon—no sooner full than it begins to wane. Such cynicism!

Honeypot

The king was in his counting-house
Counting out his money;
The queen was in the parlour
Eating bread and honey;

Sing a Song of Sixpence,
Tommy Thumb's Pretty Song Book

From 1790 in England, silver honeypots were in the shape of beehives, and about thirty years later glass pots were manufactured with silver lids that were beehive shaped. Victorian silversmiths revived these pots.

Honeypot is also the name of a children's game in which one player called the honeypot sits on his clasped hands. The other players, the honey merchants, lift him by the armpits as if they were handles and carry him to market. Their object is to make him let go of his clasp, and to this end they shake him vigorously.

Lore

Christian
Bees were considered to be holy because they swarmed out of Paradise in disgust at the Fall of Man.

When Jesus washed in the River Jordan, the bright drops that fell from his hands turned into bees that started to fly away, until He ordered them to stay and work for man.

St. Ambrose is the patron saint of beekeepers, and earned this position because of a legend that a swarm of bees settled on his mouth when he lay in his cradle as a babe.

Eastern

Vedic law decreed that a newborn boy had to be fed with butter and honey and his lips touched with a golden spoon.

In some parts of India the bridegroom is fed with honey on his wedding day to ensure fertility.

Mohammed said that the bee was the only living creature to whom God spoke.

European

The idea of telling the bees about the death of the head of the household originates from the belief that they were men's souls, and if not informed about the new master they would fly off to heaven to seek for the old one. Some people now feel it is necessary to tell the bees in their hives about all important events in the family, even a picnic excursion for which good weather is requested.

The Spanish patron saint of bees is St. John of the Nettles. Women visit his tomb to pray for a male child.

In Southern and Central Europe it used to be forbidden to feed honey to the seriously ill as this would cause the bees to die.

Zosim was the pagan bee god of the Russians, and in the Ukraine the patront saint of beekeeping is St. Sossima.

Southern Germans used always to decorate their beehives when there was a wedding, so that the bees could join in the celebrations.

The threshold of a Croatian bridegroom's home was always coated with honey before his bride crossed it for the first time.

Greek and Roman

The Greeks called bees Birds of the Muse, because of their power to confer the gift of eloquence or song by touching an infant's lips. Plato, Sophocles, and Virgil were said to have been thus blest. Offerings to the Muses consisted of wheat kneaded with honey, and libations were a mixture of water, milk, and honey.

Melissa was a Cretan nymph who helped her sister Amalthea to feed the infant Zeus on honey and goat's milk. Melissa is the Greek word for bee, and Zeus rather ungratefully turned her into one.

Callisto was another unfortunate nymph, and she was changed into a bear by Artemis for actually enjoying a fate worse than death, during a festival night in honor of the goddess, with carousing young gods and satyrs. Condemned to a furry existence, she lived in the forest on fruits and honeycombs. Pooh's distant ancestress?

Sailors from the Isle of Ortiga used to sail to the extent of the shine radiating from the shield of Athena atop her temple, and then offer oil and honey to the gods before venturing further on the sea.

Pliny imagined that honey was either the sweat of the skies or the saliva of the stars. His mind was not made up on this.

Maeterlinck

In his famous book *The Life of the Bee*, Maurice Maeterlinck compares the organization of the bee system with that of Man:

> Just as it is written in the tongue, the stomach

and mouth of the bee that it must make honey, so is it written in our eyes, our ears, our nerves, our marrow, in every lobe of our head, in the whole nervous system of our body, that we have been created in order to transform all that we absorb of the things of earth into a particular energy, of a quality unique on this globe.

And again:

The bees know not whether they will eat the honey they harvest, as we know not who will profit by the spiritual substance we introduce into the universe. As they go from flower to flower collecting more honey than themselves and their offspring can need, let us go from reality to reality seeking food for the incomprehensible flame, and, certain of having fulfilled our organic duty, prepare ourselves thus for whatever befall.

Mead

There's the clip clop of horses on the sunhoneyed
cobbles of the humming streets.

Under Milk Wood,
Dylan Thomas

Mead has been brewed worldwide since very early ages, and was probably the tipple of Dionysius or Bacchus before the cultivation of the vine. The various mythological connections of bees with the immortals would have caused beverages made from honey to be important, even sacred, to be used in offerings and libations to the gods.

In Ancient Greece the mead drink was known as Hydromel, and it had the happy property of being able to disperse anger, sadness, and afflictions of the mind. Other honey beverages were known as Ompacomel, which was made with fermented grape juice and honey; Oenomel, from pure grape juice and honey; Conditum, which was honey mixed with wine and pepper; and the famous Oxymel, made from honey, vinegar, sea salt, and rainwater. The main ailments these were used to alleviate were those of a rheumatic nature. The well-known honey wine of Ancient Rome was Muslum, and Russia was famous for its Lipez.

Chaucer's mead was called Piment or Clarre, a mixture of honey, wine, and spices. Piment was popular with kings and nobles. Morat was another liquor of this type, and it contained mulberry juice. Mead in the 16th and 17th centuries in England was a beautiful pale gold color and it sparkled like champagne.

At the present time in England there are well-known experts of mead brewing, some private and some commercial. One of the latter uses 250,000 lbs. of honey in its annual manufacture.

The name for mead seems to vary little throughout the world. In Germany it is called *Meth*, in Greece *Methu*, in India *Madhu*, and in Lithuania *Medus*. In Old Irish it used to be called *Mid*.

Nectar

Only bees can transform nectar collected from many different flowers into the truly important food we know as honey. Nectar is a sweet solution of water that contains mineral salts, gums, aromatic oils, fat, and albumen. The sugar is mostly sucrose (as found in cane and beet).

When the worker bee has sucked out the nectar and directed it into her honey stomach, a little is taken further into her personal stomach for nourishment. She then returns to the hive and regurgitates the nectar for processing by younger workers known as household bees. Both during the flight home and after this takeover, an enzyme called invertase is added to the nectar. The handling of the nectar by the household workers is carried out in order to evaporate excess moisture, and when the substance has thickened sufficiently and the sucrose has been converted into dextrose and levulose, and has become honey, it is packed into the wax cells of the comb and later covered with a thin wax cap.

Pollen is also collected from the flowers, and is transported in special sacs on the back legs of the bees. It forms the larger part of bee-bread, which is the food of workers and drones. A certain amount goes into the honey, and the more there is the better the flavor.

Bee orchid

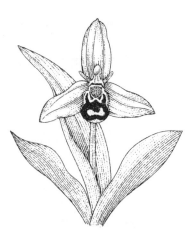

Plant cures

When honey is added to brews or decoctions of herbs, an enhanced product results. The virtues of the herbs and the honey amalgamate most happily, the honey often helping to disguise the flavor of a particular herb that may not be very palatable. The following are examples of ancient and modern remedies:

Bistory (*Polygonum bistorta*) and **Pellitory** (*Parietaria officinalis*) roots pounded and mixed with burnt alum, then made into a paste with honey, was a cure for toothache. It was packed into the cavity, a practice that doesn't bear thinking about!

Garlic mixed with honey used to be a cure for asthma, tuberculosis, whooping cough, and bronchitis.

Lettuce was preserved by the Romans in vinegar and honey and the mixture was called oxmel. They used it in cases of insomnia, constipation, poor lactation, and pain relief.

Mousear (*Hieracium pilosella*) when mixed in an infusion with honey will relieve the whooping cough.

Parsley seed beaten up with snails in their shells and mixed with honey was a secret cure for stones in the bladder during the 18th century. The inventor was a woman, to whom the government of the day paid the amazing sum of £5,000 for the recipe.

Parsley honey is useful in the treatment of indigestion, and also heart and kidney disorders. It is made by cutting up a large handful of parsley, including the roots. Wash well and put in a pan with slightly less than a quart of boiling water. Boil until a third of the liquid is left. Strain and add 500 grams or more of pure honey and boil again for fifteen minutes. Children seem to like this great provider of Vitamin C.

Poplar leaves in bud, when bruised and mixed with honey, were used to cure poor eyesight.

Radish juice is good for coughs and hoarseness. It is simple to make a dose at a time by hollowing out a large radish and filling it with honey. After three hours there will be enough juice ready for use.

Red rose petals with their white ends trimmed off may be chopped finely and simmered in honey until a sweet odor and good red color are obtained. This syrup used to be called melrosette, and is an excellent internal cleanser.

Rue boiled in equal quantities of wine and honey was prescribed by Culpeper as a cure for worms.

Sage may be used to alleviate the unpleasant effects of shingles, without interfering with treatment prescribed by doctors. Cover a handful of the herb with warm water. Let this stand covered for half an hour. Sweeten with honey to taste, and take a teaspoon every hour. If dry sage is used, it must be simmered in the water for ten minutes.

Pollen & hayfever

In addition to taking nectar from flowers, bees carry away pollen in the special sacs they have on their back legs. It forms part of their own diet, and a certain amount goes into the honey that is stored in the combs.

Pollen can be used for the treatment of hay fever, among other disorders, and it is also recommended that a potential sufferer should chew honeycomb or cappings of the cells daily for a month before the hay fever season begins. During an acute attack the dose has to be increased. The idea is that the pollen which is present in the wax will immunize the system. If the wax comes from local hives the results should be more successful, because pollen from the same flowers that trigger off the attack will be present. It works like an inoculation.

Propolis

Propolis is the resinous substance surrounding leaf buds, particularly those of poplars, and it is collected by bees to be used both as a natural cement in the maintenance of their hives and as an antibiotic for hygienic purposes within their crowded community. They use it to seal up all gaps in the hive and to secure the combs to the roof. A comb that is full of honey and that has to bear the weight of countless bees at work on it is very heavy, so the manner in which it is fastened has to be strong.

It is interesting to note that the word propolis comes from two Greek words meaning *defenses before a town*. Bees often use it for its literal meaning and place it just inside the entrance of the hive to act as a decontamination curtain.

Sometimes foreign creatures make their way into a hive, but they are very soon stung to death and carried outside if they are not too heavy for the bees. If this should be the case, as with a mouse, the body will be covered with a film of propolis to prevent decomposition from infecting the hive.

Propolis is now used by man for the treatment of such ailments as cystitis, halitosis, and throat and ear infections.

Purity

Honey as it comes from the hive, if examined under a microscope, will be seen to contain many impurities. There may be portions of dead bees, comb fragments, sand, bee hairs, and an excess of pollen grains. There may even be ash present if a smoker has been careless.

For this reason honey must be kept in a tank after extraction from the hive, so that light impurities may rise to the top and heavier ones sink to the bottom. Such a ripener tank will be fitted with a correctly placed tap with a coarse strainer. If honey is too zealously further strained through fine cloth, much nutritionally valuable content can be lost, such as necessary pollen grains, enzymes, specks of wax—natural impurities.

Dirty honey ferments, so all containers must be sterilized, and exposure to air avoided as much as possible. Honey that is taken too early from the hive, before it is sufficiently ripe, will ferment because it contains too much water.

It is therefore prudent to consider which countries one is happy to consider when buying honey. If a country of origin is not noted for general standards of hygiene, its honey should be shunned. A saying exists that only the honey from one's native land will do one any good—advice that supports the warning about imported honeys. The tiny island of Niue in the South Pacific claims to produce the purest honey in the world on its ten square miles.

Honey is often adulterated to give greater quantity by the addition of starch, glucose, gypsum, or water.

There are three main grades:

Virgin, or superfine.
Common, or yellow.
Brown.

The differences are due to the amount of pressure and exposure to heat during extraction operations.

"The Queen Bee" (Grimm)

The three sons of a king set out to seek their fortune in the world. The youngest is good and kind, and when they come across an ant hill he dissuades his brothers from destroying it. Later he saves some ducks swimming on a lake from the unkind attentions of the other sons. Finally, when they discover a bees' nest in a tree and see the honey dripping from it, he stops them from smoking out the bees. "Leave the little creatures alone," he says. "I will not suffer them to be stifled."

They proceed on their travels and discover an enchanted castle where the occupants have been turned to stone, even the horses in the stables. However, an old man has escaped the spell, and he shows them a tablet of stone on which are written the three tasks that must be successfully performed to cancel out the enchantment.

The eldest son undertakes the first task: to collect the thousand pearls belonging to the princesses of the castle and which have been scattered under the forest moss. Nine hundred and ninety-nine will not suffice, and failure will turn the seeker into stone. The unfortunate fellow can only find one hundred, and he is turned to stone. The second brother finds a mere two hundred, and joins the first in stony form. When the youngest begins the search he is in despair, but the ant king arrives with five thousand ants to forage for every single pearl. This is a reward for the protection he gave them.

The next task is to fish out the key of the princesses' bedroom from the bottom of the lake. In this instance it is the grateful ducks who come to his aid.

The final test is the hardest: to choose the youngest of the three identically beautiful princesses. There is just one small difference: each one, before falling into a sleep of stone, ate a different sweetmeat. One ate sugar, the second syrup, and the youngest honey. Once again the youngest son is in despair, until the queen bee whose hive he saved from destruction arrives to help him. She samples the lips of the three princesses and settles on the mouth of the one who has taken honey, the youngest. This makes it clear which girl is to be chosen.

The spell is thus broken. Everyone awakes from their long sleep, and the youngest prince and youngest princess are married and later become king and queen of the land.

The story ends with a typically censorious remark by the authors: "And the other two brothers had to put up with the other two sisters."

Recipes

Edinburgh Egg Nog

1 egg

1 teaspoon honey

½ cup milk

⅛ teaspoon ground ginger

⅛ teaspoon powdered cinnamon

2 teaspoons rum or brandy

Separate the egg, and beat white until stiff. Add honey and beat in well. Beat together egg yolk, milk, spices, and rum or brandy. Fold in stiff white. Serve in tall glass for the best pick-me-up.

Honey Roast Lamb

1 teaspoon dry mustard

4 tablespoons honey

Mix ingredients together and spread over joint of lamb before roasting.

Orange Honey Sauce

½ cup honey

¼ cup orange juice

1 teaspoon grated orange peel

Mix until well blended. Serve on sponge desserts or ice cream.

Sweet and Sour Cabbage

1 small white cabbage

2 tablespoons honey

2 oz. butter

2 tablespoons lemon juice

¼ teaspoon caraway seeds

Shred cabbage roughly. Cook rapidly in covered pan of boiling salted water. Drain after 10 minutes or when tender. Add other ingredients. Cook gently for 5 minutes, stirring from time to time. Enough for four people. Also good cold.

Honey Salad Dressing

4 tablespoons clear liquid honey

8 fluid oz. olive oil

½ pint wine vinegar

Put in blender for one minute.

A Pink Salad Cream

⅓ cup liquid honey

1 teaspoon salt

1 teaspoon dry mustard

1 teaspoon celery salt

1 teaspoon paprika

1 teaspoon onion juice

$\frac{1}{4}$ teaspoon lemon juice

1 cup sunflower oil

$\frac{1}{4}$ cup wine or honey vinegar

Mix all ingredients except oil and vinegar. Add oil and vinegar slowly and alternately in blender. (If oil and vinegar are beaten into the mixture it will tend to separate with standing.) This dressing will keep for at least a month in a stoppered jar.

Apricot Layer

$\frac{1}{2}$ cup dried apricots

$\frac{1}{2}$ cup cold water

2 tablespoons honey

$\frac{1}{2}$ cup whipping cream

Soak apricots in water until soft. Put with honey in blender. Blend for a few seconds. Add cream and blend until mixture is fluffy. May be used as top layer of a plain cake, or a sauce over ice cream, or other suitable dessert.

Honey and Yogurt Cheesecake

8 oz. almond macaroons

3 oz. melted butter

5 oz. natural yogurt

8 oz. cottage cheese

2 tablespoons liquid honey

Grated rind of one orange

Break macaroons with rolling pin. Stir in melted butter and press into 8 in. pastry shell. Chill. Mix yogurt, cottage cheese, honey, and orange rind. Fill into crumb case. Chill for 1 hour. Decorate with crystallized orange slices.

Honey Fudge

$\frac{1}{4}$ pint top of milk

Small tin condensed milk (sweetened)

4 oz. butter or margarine

2 tablespoons clear liquid honey

1 lb. confectioner's sugar

Pinch of cream of tartar

Mix all ingredients in heavy-based saucepan. Bring slowly to the boil while stirring. Then boil fast, stirring occasionally, for about 8 minutes (until a small amount dropped into water forms a soft ball—240 F). Remove pan from heat. Cool slightly, then beat mixture until thick. Pour into greased shallow tin. Leave until nearly set. Mark into squares. When quite set separate pieces and leave to harden on a rack.

Honey Cake

6 oz. plain flour

3 eggs

2 oz. fat

2 oz. sugar

4 oz. honey

4 oz. dried fruit

Simply cream together all the ingredients and put into a 6 in. tin. Bake at 350 F for 1 hour. Reduce to 325 F until cooked through.

Baklava

1 lb. puff pastry or strudel leaves

For filling:

$\frac{3}{4}$ cup sugar

$1\frac{1}{2}$ cups unsalted melted butter

1 cup chopped or ground almonds

2 cups chopped or ground walnuts

$\frac{1}{2}$ teaspoon cinnamon

$\frac{1}{4}$ teaspoon nutmeg

For syrup:

$1\frac{1}{2}$ cups honey

$\frac{3}{4}$ cup sugar

Short cinnamon stick

$\frac{1}{2}$ a sliced orange

$\frac{1}{2}$ a sliced lemon

Roll out pastry as thinly as possible. Cut into pieces to fit a 15 × 12 in. tin. Set aside.

Make syrup by boiling sugar and honey with $\frac{3}{4}$ cup of water. Add cinnamon and sliced fruit. Reduce heat and simmer for 10 minutes. Strain. Cool.

Combine walnuts, almonds, sugar, and spices for the filling. Set aside.

Assembly: Put 2 pieces of pastry into base of tin. Brush liberally with melted butter. Sprinkle with nut filling. Continue alternating in this way, ending with pastry layer. Use a sharp knife to cut through *top layer only* in diagonal and parallel lines, crossing these to mark out diamond shapes.

Bake at 325 F for 1 hour till golden and puffed up. Turn off the heat, and leave tin for a further hour in oven.

Remove and pour cool syrup over the hot Baklava. Cut right through the diamond patterns to make about 36 pieces. Leave to cool in tin and soak up the syrup.

This is not as difficult as it may sound, and is well worth trying for the acclaim that is bound to ensue!

Bread

½ lb. oatmeal

1 pint milk

4 teaspoons dried yeast

20 oz. whole wheat flour

20 oz. white flour

2 tablespoons salt

4 oz. butter

2 teaspoons sugar

2 tablespoons honey

Put milk and oatmeal to soak for about 3 hours. Add yeast and sugar to ½ pint warm water and stir. Leave for 10 minutes. Mix flour and salt. Warm butter and honey in a pan, and pour onto the flour, yeast, and water. Add soaked oatmeal and mix to form a dough. Knead for about 10 minutes. Leave to double for 1½ hours. Knead for 5 minutes and divide into loaves. Prove for up to 1½ hours. Bake on 450 F for 10 minutes. Reduce to 350 F and continue baking for 30 minutes.

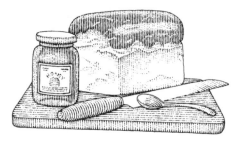

Royal jelly

Royal jelly is made exclusively for the feeding of baby queens in the hive. It is so potent that it evolves a queen bee from just the same egg that otherwise would develop into a worker bee. The quantity to be found in any hive is surprisingly small, an observation that stresses its great power.

If it works such wonders for bees, can it not be used to help humans? Scientific investigation has led to the marketing of beauty creams claiming to rejuvenate aging skins, and of elixirs and tonics. As the jelly is composed of a particular female hormone, research has taken place to determine the possibility of its use in contraceptives and the treatment of infertility. The big drawback lies in the fact that it deteriorates quickly once it is taken out of the hive, but it can be preserved for some time in honey or in mead. Another disadvantage, of course, lies in the very small quantities available, and this factor contributes to the high cost of manufacturing anything containing this wonder substance.

Shakespeare's hive

In *King Henry V*, Shakespeare has the Archbishop of Canterbury compare the state of man with the organization of a beehive, thus:

> For so work the honey bees,
> Creatures that by a rule in nature teach
> The act of order to a peopled kingdom.
> They have a king and officers of sorts;

Where some, like magistrates, correct at home,
Others, like merchants, venture trade abroad,
Others, like soldiers, armed in their stings,
Make boot upon the summer's velvet buds;
Which pillage they with merry march bring home
To the tent-royal of their emperor:
Who, busied in his majesty, surveys
The singing masons building roofs of gold,
The civil citizens kneading up the honey,
The poor mechanic porters crowding in
Their heavy burdens at his narrow gate,
The sad-ey'd justice, with his surly hum,
Delivering o'er to executors pale
The lazy yawning drone.

Here all the tasks of the inhabitants are dramatically and vividly set out; but there is no mention of any females, and at the center is a king or emperor, not a queen. It was the Dutch natural historian Jan Swammerdam, born in 1637, who finally established the sex with the aid of the early microscope, and got the idea officially accepted. Earlier suggestions about queens, made in different countries, had never been taken seriously.

Shopping for honey

The Owl and the Pussy-cat went to sea
In a beautiful pea-green boat.
They took some honey, and plenty of money,
Wrapped up in a five-pound note.

> The Owl and the Pussy-cat,
> *Edward Lear*

Apart from the different flavored honeys we can find in the shops, we can expect to find the following types:

Liquid: as it comes from hives.

Natural crystallized: liquid honey, matured.

Soft-set: crystallized honey chopped and mixed with liquid honey, then re-set. It never re-crystallizes after this process.

Cut comb: small slabs of honeycomb placed in containers.

Section honey: worked and produced by the bees within wooden frames supplied to them in the hives.

Chunk honey: pieces of honeycomb floating in jars of liquid honey.

Singing hinny

A singing hinny is a rich griddle cake that seems to sing as it cooks. It is enriched with mead, and hinny is a derivation of the word honey.

Smoking

Cigarettes can be manufactured without tobacco content or nicotine in any form from natural aromatic herbs mixed with honey. To be in a room where such a cigarette is being smoked is to be aware of a pleasant fragrance at first. Later, one starts to wonder where the nearby bonfire is. There is the sweetly acrid smell of burning greenstuff. The smoker, however, continues to enjoy the herbal aroma and the blissfully virtuous feeling that the nicotine habit has been kicked.

Statistics

Bees and honey—cockney rhyming slang for money

There are 500 bees in the world for every human being, and they produce 500,000 tons of honey a year.

One gallon of nectar gives energy for a bee to cruise four million miles at seven miles an hour.

A bee makes 2,000 forays to flowers to produce just a thimbleful of honey.

37,000 loads of nectar are needed to make 1 lb. of honey, involving some 148,000 miles. It would take a bee thirty-five to forty years to do this—if it could live that long.

To produce 100 lbs. of honey surplus for man, a bee colony will use up about 500 lbs. plus 100 lbs. of pollen.

The greatest reported amount of wild honey ever extracted from a single hive is 404 lbs. on 29 August 1974 in Santa Cruz, California.

A queen multiplies its weight in the larval stage—five days—by 1,500 times, on its diet of royal jelly.

Rudolf Steiner

Rudolf Steiner, philosopher and scientist, says of bees:

> With the exception of the queen, the bees are actually beings which, as I would like to put it, say to themselves: *We will renounce the individual sexual life that we make ourselves bearers of love.* Thus they have been able to bring what lives in the flowers into the hive; and when you begin really to think this out rightly, you will reach the whole mystery of the beehive.
>
> The life of this sprouting, budding love which is in the flowers is there too, within the honey. You

can also study what honey does when you eat it yourself. What does the honey do? When honey is eaten it furthers the right connection in man between the airy and the watery elements. Nothing is better for man than to add the right proportion of honey to his food. For in a wonderful way the bees see to it that man learns to work with his soul upon the organs of his body. In the honey the bee gives back again to man what he needs to further the activity of his soul-forces within his body. Thus when man adds some honey to his food, he wishes so to prepare his soul that it may work rightly within his body—breathe rightly.

Beekeeping is therefore something that greatly helps to advance our civilization, for it makes men strong . . . When one stands before a hive of bees one should say quite solemnly to oneself: *By way of the beehive the whole Cosmos enters man and makes him strong and able.*

Although the above is a mystical explanation, it is worthy of careful consideration. Most people have to admit that there is something about honey that has not been defined, that cannot be discovered by chemical analysis. It certainly benefits the human body today as in the distant past, as we may realize when we study current health-food literature and the many instances of folklore and mythology that feature this wonderful food of Nature.

Marna Pease, who translated Rudolf Steiner's nine lectures on bees which he delivered in 1923, had a profound knowledge of beekeeping and bee lore, and was the author of *Honey as a Food and as a Remedy*. Of honey, she said: "The more honey is used as a food, the less it will be needed as a remedy."

Stings

Bees are said to be so moral that they concentrate on stinging fornicators!

They hate human perspiration, and in hot weather will attack the wrists, neck, and foreheads of sweaty people. They also dislike the smell of alcohol, perfumed cosmetics such as after-shave, hair lacquer, and the scent we put behind our ears. All this seems to present a picture of beekeepers as frustrated and ill-groomed people—an image far removed from the truth!

Storage

All pure honey will granulate, and there is absolutely no difference in its quality. Granulated honey may be returned to a clear state by gentle heating, but care should be taken that the heating is as low as possible so that nothing in the valuable content is destroyed.

Honey will darken with age, but if properly ripened before gathering it will keep for five years in airtight and cool conditions. It should be stored in bulk and in stone or earthenware containers. The acids it contains will attack metal.

Honey is hygroscopic, which is a complicated way of saying that it has the power to attract and absorb moisture from anything nearby. It is for this reason that it should be kept in air-tight containers. If it absorbs too much moisture it will soon ferment, and it is said that the first alcohol was discovered when a jar of honey was left out in the rain by chance, and the contents consumed—with strange results.

Survival

We'll sit contentedly
And eat our pot of honey on the grave.

Modern Love,
George Meredith

It has already been mentioned that our survival on earth depends on the job of pollination the bees perform on plants that provide our food. It has now been proved that they have even further know-how. They can resist the fatal effects of radiation fall-out. We must find out how they do it. Our civil defense workers should get themselves to the nearest beehive!

Sweet tooth

The Vitamin K that is contained in honey has among its functions that of preventing acid bacteria forming in the mouth. This acid causes tooth decay and is produced chiefly when sugar is eaten. So it makes sense, when a craving for something sweet overcomes us, to make for the honeypot wherein lies both sweetness and an inbuilt protection.